Rylant, Cynthia.
Ludie's life

Ludie's Life

CYNTHIA RYLANT

Ludie's Life

Harcourt, Inc.

Orlando Austin New York San Diego Toronto London

www.HarcourtBooks.com

Library of Congress Cataloging-in-Publication Data
Rylant, Cynthia.
Ludie's life/Cynthia Rylant.
p. cm.
1. Poor women—Poetry.   2. West Virginia—Poetry.
3. Women—West Virginia—Poetry.   I. Title.
PS3568.Y55L83 2006
811'.54—dc22   2005014231
ISBN-13: 978-0-15-205389-5   ISBN-10: 0-15-205389-1

Text set in Garamond MT
Designed by April Ward

First edition
H G F E D C B A

Printed in the United States of America

For Elda, Velma, Agnes...
and all the Ludies who raised me

Ludie's Life

Would she tell you that six children

were too many,

that some disappointed,

others surprised,

but that, all in all,

six

were too many

and one

would have been just fine?

Would she tell you that she married

that boy at fifteen

not only because he was tall and kind

but also because

she needed a way out?

Her mother had died years before,

her father married again,

a woman with children of her own,

a woman who pushed Ludie

away from the house,

away from the supper table.

Would she tell you that she stole food

when she was eight,
stole food from the supper table
and ran to the creek to eat it,
because had she waited for that woman
to feed her,
there would have been
only scraps?
Ludie was a beautiful girl,
saucy, some called her,
and she raised herself,
herself and her sister, Trula,
after their mother died.
They were living in Alabama,
it was the 1910s,
and there was a train to Birmingham,
a train that could take them out of that
coal camp
to Birmingham
if only they'd had the money
and the courage,
but the train to Birmingham
always left without them.

They sat on the grassy hill

with everyone else

who had come to watch the train

pull in and out,

not a nickel in

their pockets,

owned by the mine

that sent their fathers and sons

to dark graves.

Not a nickel in

their pockets.

Ludie's life then was happy and sad,

she would say.

There was no thought

to what work

she might do in her life.

Teacher.

Nurse.

Not a chance.

Not when you're stealing food

off your own supper table.

Did Ludie's father

love her?
Obviously not as much
as the second woman
he married.
This was not lost
on Ludie.
So when that boy—
they called him "Rupe,"
and he was tall and kind—
walked her home from the train
when she was fifteen,
their future was sealed
and there would be six babies,
maybe five too many,
and sex
would never be what it was
that first night,
it would be instead
one of those gifts
you know you can't afford
but you spend the money anyway,
sex would be instead

one of those things
you could have done without, maybe,
if you'd known the cost.
She spent the money anyway
and there were six babies,
five too many,
and she'd be the rest of her life
taking care of them
in one way or another,
taking care of them
until her last breath
because that's the way it was,
people needed Ludie
all the way to the end.
Never a time
when she wasn't doing for somebody.
And did anyone know
what she could have been?
Did that award for Sunday-school teacher,
that commemorative plate of *The Last Supper*
she received in her middle age,
did that tell them

what she could have been?
Because she loved teaching.
She taught the Young People's Class,
teenagers without an interest, really,
they'd rather be playing ball or dancing,
she taught them the Bible
and they quieted
and listened
and years later some would seek her out,
still living in that little house
in the country,
old now,
both her and the house,
and, all grown up,
somebody would tell her
what she'd done,
the difference she'd made
in a teenager's life,
and isn't this
what makes a person important,
that years later
someone seeks you out

to say thank you?
Did anyone know how
Ludie loved teaching,
how she loved the language
of the King James Bible
and that those were her
happiest years,
six children grown,
and teaching.
But she never forgot
stealing those scraps off the dinner table
and ever after,
all her life,
she would avoid anyone who had
more than she,
who had bettered themselves,
anyone who was uppity.
Don't mention that
so-and-so
had accomplished
this or that
if it involved anything out

of Ludie's reach.
Brick houses,
college educations.
Success.
Ludie never learned to drive,
lived half her life
without indoor plumbing,
and knew the pain of being more
than the world would ever see,
knew the pain
of being bright
and funny
and even philosophical
but without a brick house,
a college education.
She didn't want to be reminded,
so she stayed away
from the funeral parlor
if the dead relative
had done well in life,
made a little money.
Ludie didn't want to show up

and have to tolerate the distant cousins,
with nice suits and ties
and better cars
and houses in town,
treating her like the poor relation
she was.
She stayed in the country
and read the King James Bible,
where no one within a stone's throw
was better than she.
Poverty is hardest
on those intelligent enough
to understand it.
"Poor but happy."
Ludie would hear it
again and again in her life,
but she was never happy
that way,
she was more than that,
so she stayed away from the funeral parlors
where they might try to tell her
who she wasn't.

When they were first married,

Ludie and Rupe lived with her father.

That didn't last long.

Rupe got a better job

up in the West Virginia mines,

and they left Alabama for good.

Ludie never looked back.

Some of her relatives followed them.

Trula and her young husband.

Rupe's sister and her young husband.

They'd all stick together,

and no one would starve.

Someone else came up to West Virginia, too.

Rupe's crazy brother, Cal.

Cal was a man just teetering on the line

between good and bad.

No one knew for sure

if he was crazy or just plain mean.

This much is true:

Ludie feared him.

And he came to live with them,

with Ludie and Rupe,

in that camp house in West Virginia,

and when Rupe was away at the mine all day,

it was just Ludie and Cal

there at the house, with the babies.

Ludie always kept her eye on the door.

Cal had good days

and bad days,

and Ludie trusted him on none of them.

When she had to go to the basement to bathe,

she took the butcher knife.

Sometimes he'd go off hitchhiking

and they'd wonder for weeks where he was,

then back home he'd come,

crazy grin.

Cal got tuberculosis

and he had to go live in the sanatorium

in Beckley.

Ludie prayed to God to forgive her

for being so happy.

She put the knife away

and smiled

and prayed to God.

When Cal finally got out, after a couple of years,

he was a changed man.

Quiet. Unsure.

The grin had disappeared.

Ludie took pity on him.

She invited him to walk with her

to the mailbox every day,

and they took the old beagle

and sometimes the neighbor's mutt came along,

and on these walks

they talked about Alabama,

what they remembered of it,

who they'd hated,

who they'd loved,

and speculated on how everybody had ended up.

Such things happen,

this reaching for someone

who has known who you have been.

Ludie realized she preferred the company of

her crazy brother-in-law

to that of any of the perfectly sane

Methodists
living out on the hard road.
Cal was family,
he *knew* her,
and she was willing
to be a little afraid of him,
in order to feel
so safe.

Alabama was hot in summer,

warm in winter,

and the mosquitoes never left.

It was all Ludie had known,

she was used to this,

and each year undulated

in its long, lazy haze.

Then she moved to West Virginia.

Did she think she was dreaming

when she first saw the trees in October?

Did something like

joy

leap into her throat?

There is nothing so beautiful in Alabama as this,

she must have said,

gazing at the scarlet hills.

Then winter arrived one night,

when she wasn't expecting it.

Ludie rose and looked out her window.

A silent snow had drifted itself up to her door,

the windowsills,

and, at one corner of the house,
all the way up to the eaves.
Rupe lay sleeping, unaware.
The babies slept, unaware.
Ludie looked out her window at this new world,
and in that moment
she knew what it was to let go of oneself.
Understood, finally, the apostles
who died for something as deeply quiet and certain
as this,
her first snow.

Ludie loved the coal camp in Jonben.

There in the soft green mountains of West Virginia,

nestled between the ridges,

she settled into Jonben with Rupe and her babies

and found out who she was.

Ludie was happy there

and the world could carry on with its business,

its war and its money,

its pain and its suffering;

and she would instead remain here

in the clean white-painted house

with a front porch and a well out back,

enough room for a garden and chickens,

and sunrise out the window

when she rose up with Rupe

to make his breakfast,

filling his lunch pail

before she nursed the baby

and wiped the small faces

of the other children,

warm and sweaty with sleep.

Ludie loved the coal camp in Jonben.
Her sister and sister-in-law were there
and the children ran back and forth,
one house to another,
while the women cooked
and mopped
and sewed
and mopped again.
Coal dust was always a problem,
coming in with the men.
But Ludie's house was clean,
beds made,
tables dusted;
she would not live like trash.
She still loved Rupe, even after all the babies,
and she waited up for him,
those nights when he needed to stay in the mine
to load that last car with coal,
unable to come home until he'd met his quota.
He was losing his hair,
a balding thirty-year-old,
but she didn't mind.

He was still funny and strong.

He drank some on the weekends,

the way miners do,

but what could she say about that?

When she spent her days a mile below in three feet

of cold water,

chipping away at rock,

then she could say something about that.

Miners died,

and often.

But they weren't the only casualties of coal-camp life.

Everything was precarious.

One little girl caught on fire in her house,

too close to the stove,

and ran, burning,

to the next house for help,

dead when she got there.

There were those

who were careless with guns.

And those deliberate with them.

There was influenza

and tuberculosis

and emphysema.

Life was precarious.

But Ludie was happy.

Still pretty, in her loose cotton dresses,

soft long hair,

she knew who she was.

And she had this sense

that this was beautiful,

this place and time.

She loved wash day because she could be outside,

a reason to be outside,

the smell of maple leaves and honeysuckle in the air,

a blue sky,

the freshness of soap,

and the satisfaction of crisp hot shirts on the line.

She was not trapped here.

She was not lost.

And did she ever wish to be someone else,

a woman in furs in New York City,

or, closer to home,

the mine owner's wife?

She knew who she was.

The cooking,

the babies, the washing,

waiting up for Rupe until two in the morning.

No, she never wanted anything but this.

She woke up every day

and never wondered

what she'd find to do with herself,

never wondered

why she'd been born in the first place,

did not lie in bed

and fret about the life she should have been living

instead of this one.

She would grow older

and her children and grandchildren

would try on this job and that one,

this wife and that one,

a different town,

a different country,

never really sure about who they were

and what they were meant for.

But until she was ninety,

sitting on a porch and no one stopping by,

Ludie would never doubt that
she was worthy of life,
God's child,
and necessary.

This was the rule in Ludie's house:

Do not sit on the beds.

Do NOT sit on the beds.

It was tempting.

Every child in the house

wanted to sit on the beds.

But Ludie cared about the beauty of things.

What little she had,

she cared about.

And her small house,

the final one she lived in for over forty years,

mattered.

It had been a one-room schoolhouse.

It was not meant to be a home.

But the man who'd owned it before

had cut it up into the essential rooms for habitation:

a living room,

a kitchen,

three tiny bedrooms.

A bathroom back then

was not even a passing thought.

And to get to Ludie's kitchen from the living room,
a person had to walk through a bedroom.
There was no way
around it.
One would make
a left
and walk through a bedroom.
Or make a right
and walk through a bedroom.
But bypassing a bedroom was not an option
to get to the kitchen.
Ludie thus cared how her beds looked.
People came through every day.
If the preacher stopped by,
he'd be squeezing past a bed,
just like anybody else.
So no one sat on the beds.
Ludie did not want even a hint
of shabbiness in her home.
The beds were clean and smooth,
the dressing tables decorated with doilies,
even the Kleenex holders were crocheted.

Ludie loved this home,
the old wardrobe she and Rupe had
bought at the company store,
the big RCA console TV,
her red swivel-rocker.
She loved
the yellow refrigerator
and the fancy wooden potato bin
where she kept her cornflakes.
Ludie dusted everything in the house
with lemon Pledge,
and she ran the sweeper every week,
and she never went to bed
with a dirty dish in the sink.
Putting away,
wiping off,
straightening up:
ordered,
in God's universe.

When Ludie was still having her babies,
doctors rode out on horses to handle the delivery,
and there was no hope of a hospital
if something went wrong,
so everyone prayed to God it wouldn't
while the poor woman moaned
and the old women
moved beside her like ghosts.
Ludie's other children were banished
to a relative's house for the occasion,
where they were fed biscuits and molasses
and told everything would be just fine.
They didn't believe it
and now and then one would wonder
what they should do,
should they pray,
should they beg for home.
These were children used to chores
and responsibility
and shouldn't they have a hand in this, they wondered.
But things continued on without them,

the camp doctor there in Ludie's house
measuring the progress of events,
and asking her
could she just push that baby a little harder,
he's almost here.
Ludie was a private person
and did not like having to suffer aloud
in the company of others,
she wanted to do this thing alone.
But every time,
every time,
she'd had to reveal herself
to the camp doctor,
to the old women,
had to show them everything of herself, in her agony,
and ever after
she would feel a small piece of her
missing
when she was in their presence.
They had seen her so wide open and helpless,
and while she was grateful to them
and told them so,

there was a part of her
wanting to just reach out
and take back that missing piece,
just reach behind their eyes
and take back that piece of her
she'd given away
as she lay there bloody and screaming
while they watched,
composed,
the next day wondering again
about the chance of rain.

There was land all around Ludie and Rupe's
house in the country.
In spring,
mornings would hum
with the sound of tractors baling hay
in the field next door.
Ludie would send one of the kids out across that field
with an empty glass jug
to buy buttermilk from the Halsteads, who kept cows.
And there were plenty of black snakes,
which liked to come out of the tall grass and
sleep under Rupe's car.
But in the 1980s
the Halsteads passed away,
and much of their land began passing, too.
Their children inherited it,
and by that time it was worth something,
so they began to sell it off
to anyone with a notion
to set up a house trailer or a tent.

The cow pastures were soon dotted
with mobile homes and aluminum outbuildings.
Some people built small wooden houses
with attached redwood decks,
plastic slicky-slides next to them.
The houses and trailers lay this way and that,
at odd angles to one another,
and property lines were nebulous.
All this was going on outside Ludie's living-room window,
and her children,
grown now and nostalgic for their old playing fields,
would stop by and complain about the new neighbors.
But Ludie was all right about it, she said.
The babies in those families
deserve to grow up in the country, too, she said.
Ludie had not learned
to be stingy about land,
and besides,
one of those new neighbors—
Stella Sommers—
had crossed that field with a blueberry cobbler

one morning

and no cow had ever come calling

with that.

Ludie liked John F. Kennedy.

Everybody in the family did.

People said West Virginia won him the election

and who would have thought

a bunch of hillbillies could do that.

But there was something about him

they trusted.

Something about him

made them think

he wouldn't come asking for votes

then turn around and make fun of them

after he left.

Ludie liked him.

And after he died,

she kept that 11x14 picture she had of

him up on the wall—

the one with the

"Ask not" quote—

for a good ten years before

she finally took it down and

hung up a thimble rack instead.

By that time his brother Bobby
had died, too,
and one of Ludie's children had married,
of all things,
a Jew,
so Ludie took down that picture
and faced the fact
that things were changing now,
and this was
a whole new world.

In 1968,

Ludie's youngest son went to Vietnam.

He'd joined the air force

and was stationed in Africa for a time.

But he was still young, still a boy.

He'd been a basketball star

at Grassy Meadows High,

he was tall like Rupe,

and people liked him

because he moved and spoke in a peaceful way

and seemed delighted by whatever the conversation

   was about.

He did not die

in Vietnam.

That's the important thing to say about him right away.

He did not die.

When he was called,

Ludie and Rupe and the rest of the family still at home,

they all went to the county airport to see him off,

when he was called to Vietnam.

A little propeller plane there on that mountaintop,

waiting to send him out to Southeast Asia,

this boy

who liked books

and played ball

and was good to his mother.

Ludie dressed up to send him off,

dressed as if for church,

or a funeral,

and she stood in her good coat and pumps

and said good-bye there on the tarmac

to her boy.

She had carried him on her hip years ago

and still remembered his small face asleep.

Ludie said good-bye to him and

gave him up,

let loose of him there,

for nothing could be done,

he was not her boy

now that the government said it owned him,

insisted that he go to Vietnam or else.

It didn't matter

who his mother was

or that they still didn't have running water
or that he'd had to hitchhike home
from every basketball practice
or that he idolized his father,
whom people called "Rupe."
Ludie gave him up
and he didn't die,
but for years she'd wake up in the night
and would think, *think,*
where was he,
and she'd remember that he didn't die,
but her heart still pounded
and she was up for the day.

Ludie was not an animal lover.

This would surprise anyone who knew her children,

especially the girls,

for they all grew into the biggest

bleeding-heart animal lovers

in the world.

Arranging their lives around

dogs and cats.

Ludie could not understand it.

Maybe, having been a

hungry child,

she had no room in her heart for pets.

Rupe kept hunting dogs,

and they let their youngest girl

have a big tomcat,

though more because of mice

than sentiment.

But Ludie could not abide

a dog in her house,

and even the cat

had to beg his way in

on ten-below nights.
Ludie could not afford
to turn animals into people.
She skinned and fried the rabbits Rupe shot.
She chopped the bushy tails off squirrels
before stewing them up.
She could wring the neck of a chicken,
pluck it,
dip into its warm belly and pull out the
soft jelly eggs
it would never lay.
There were hogs in the hog lot
waiting to be slaughtered.
And the neighbor's beef cow
looking over the fence at her every morning.
Ludie could not afford
to turn animals into people.
She'd known hunger.
She'd learned the hard way what it is
not to have a choice about food.
It is a privilege,
a certain pass

given those of a certain class,

to dote on animals.

Ludie had counted out

too many grains of rice

to care whether

the dog had enough company

or the cat

liked its food.

Maybe next life

she'd be an animal lover.

This life, not.

But there was one cat,

before Ludie died,

which worked its way

into her house.

Flick was not a beautiful cat.

And he'd had some hard knocks.

There was not a person Flick trusted

to never one day

throw him out a car window.

He'd had some hard knocks.

So when Ludie's youngest daughter moved away

and left him there
sitting in Ludie's living room,
it was not a warm communion.
Ludie ignored him
and he, in turn,
wanted nothing but out.
They circled each other for months.
Then one day Flick was nearly torn to pieces
by a pack of dogs in Ludie's yard.
Dogs who'd known Flick all his life but, somehow,
together they'd forgotten
who they were.
They attacked him.
Flick, in bits and pieces,
was rushed to the hospital
and though everyone said he'd die—
and maybe should have—
he pulled through.
Patched together, he hobbled
back into Ludie's house
and after that everything changed.
She bought him

his favorite canned food.
He slept on her bed.
In the middle of the night,
she got up to let him in or out.
Ludie could still not afford
to turn animals into people.
But she knew courage when she saw it,
and when it walked in a room,
she found it a chair.

Just when Ludie had sent

the last of her children off

and thought she was done,

three grandchildren

were dropped on her doorstep.

Never mind the reasons why,

people just trying to get their lives straight.

Ludie was by this time

tired of raising kids.

Tired of that drag on her,

hands reaching out,

and these children were worse,

for their parents had left them behind,

and there was all that grief.

One, age four, the only child of a miserable union,

suffered most.

She'd been left once before at Ludie's,

at two.

Left for a little while, not so long.

And that first night

had put herself on the floor in the corner of
the bedroom.
Face to the wall and silent.
Would not turn toward the grandmother and grandfather
standing there
trying to console her.
It nearly killed Rupe,
seeing this pitiable child
turned away from him to the wall.
A doctor's call revealed the child had an earache.
But unlike most babies
had not held out her arms for comfort.
Instead turned to the wall.
This little girl lived with Ludie now,
plus the two other grandchildren.
Ludie was good to them all.
She washed them, fed them,
clothed them, took them to church.
But there was not a day
when she didn't wish they'd go away.
She was tired of raising children.

She'd be good to them.
But she'd hold back, too.
They were, after all,
burdens.
Years and years later,
years and years,
Ludie would sit on a porch swing
and try to tell one of them,
the pitiable little girl who'd sat in a corner,
now grown,
and happy,
and a painter,
Ludie would try to tell her that she was sorry
for not wanting her back then,
for resenting the child
whose parents couldn't get things straight.
The granddaughter said she didn't know what Ludie
was talking about.
That Ludie had always been a good grandmother.
But Ludie, like most in their old age,
was remembering all the wrongs she'd done,

and not too many rights.

She had a long list of things she was sorry for.

And nothing left but words now

to make it better,

and a little time.

The mailboxes were out at the end of the road,
and until she was ninety,
Ludie walked out there every day
to get the paper.
Letters couldn't be counted on,
but the paper was rock solid.
Just the *Valley Register:*
some news, some ads,
pictures of cheerleaders,
and the obituaries.
The obituaries interested everybody,
including Ludie.
It happens in a small community.
People look to see who died
and whether they should press their
clothes for the funeral home.
There is the long list of
children and grandchildren surviving,
where they live,
and here Ludie learned a lot
about where people moved after high school

and whether they found love.

The obituaries were rarely as colorful

as, say,

those in the *New York Times*.

It's hard to compete

with Audrey Hepburn and Jacqueline Kennedy Onassis

in death.

Though Ludie would have

liked it better if someone had tried.

If someone at the *Valley Register*

had just tracked down the people who knew

the real story behind Mildred Lacey

who died in the Piney View Nursing Home

at age eighty-seven

and was preceded in death by her

beloved husband, Noah,

fourteen years earlier.

Ludie knew

there was so much more.

What kind of mother Mrs. Lacey was

or whether she got on with her children

or how long it took her to die,
when death finally started knocking.
Did Mrs. Lacey dislike football and was
she a Reds fan.
What did she think
of that new combination elementary/junior high
they just built
and did her husband drink.
There was a lot to know,
if only those fellows at the newspaper cared enough
to find it all out.
But Ludie walked to the mailbox every day
nevertheless,
with the anticipation that comes of
caring who died and
what's going on in the world.
In 1962,
the world was about ready to blow itself up,
and Ludie read of this on her way home,
about the nuclear missiles aimed her way,
the clock ticking.

Well, they'd be fine, Rupe and her.

They'd just head for the basement.

They had plenty of vegetables and potatoes in the cellar;

they'd just wait it out.

As long as no missiles landed anywhere nearby,

they'd make it,

they always had.

Nobody wanted anything from

around here anyway, she figured.

If the Russians invaded

they'd skip West Virginia,

no gold here,

just some dirt roads and people on pensions.

Ludie read about Mr. Khrushchev and the Russians,

and she did worry for those in the big cities

with nowhere to hide.

But here life would go on,

they'd maybe wait a week to sit on the porch

if there was a bomb,

but after that they'd just pick up.

The world had always run its business without them;

nobody cared about these hollows.
Ludie put the paper away
and started her beans soaking
for supper.

Ludie used a johnny house

until she was fifty-eight years old.

Then Rupe had a septic dug,

and Ludie picked out a nice blue commode.

But until she was fifty-eight,

Ludie did her business outside,

if there wasn't three feet of snow,

in which case

she used the pee pot under her bed.

Rupe never minded the johnny house

and even after they got the new indoor bathroom,

he continued using it

exclusively.

Every so often he would move

the johnny house—

dig a new hole in the yard

and set the thing on top.

And he did eventually concede

to replacing the stacks of newspapers

he'd relied on all his life

with a proper roll of toilet paper

Ludie had provided.
But though they'd been
married a long time
and usually saw things eye to eye,
when it came to where they put their bottoms,
Ludie and Rupe
parted company.
She added one of those
soft pillow seats
to the top of her blue commode
while he hunkered down onto a
piece of barn wood
with a sports page from last May.
Winter nights,
when Ludie rolled out of bed
and shuffled into the next room
in her nightgown and slippers,
Rupe just grabbed a flashlight
on his way
out the door.

After the men were finished with mining,
living now on UMWA pensions
and rattling around the house,
Ludie's sister, Trula,
moved to Roanoke,
and there followed years and years
of driving over the Blue Ridge Parkway
from one sister's place to another.
Trula and her husband, Cleo, had settled in
a small one-level house
that had two paths
running out from it,
one toward their eldest daughter
and one toward their youngest daughter.
Both daughters had children.
So when Ludie and Rupe arrived with
some of their own children and grandchildren in the car,
having spent fifteen hours balancing on the edges
of two-lane mountain roads behind coal trucks,
there was real joy,
and memories would be made.

Trula lived near enough Virginia Beach
that a day could be devoted to the ocean.
For Ludie's family it was like a chance to see heaven.
None of them ever thought they'd see the ocean.
They put everything they thought they'd need
in one of the cars,
then climbed in and went to Virginia Beach
for the day.
There is no use trying to describe
what they felt
when they got there.
Such feelings they never found words for.
No mountain child ever finds words for an ocean.
And Ludie herself never needed to.
Because Ludie never went to the ocean.
She stayed behind with Trula and Cleo
and she let the others go.
Surely someone said to her
that she must go,
at least once,
it's like nothing you've ever seen.
But she stayed behind

and gave no reason why
though one might guess
it had something to do with being poor.
The ocean is free,
a luxury everyone can afford,
but Ludie learned early on
that there is a price for everything.
What happens
when someone thinks she deserves
something like seeing the ocean?
Where does it go after that?
Ludie must have known
she would never be the same.
Her children and grandchildren weren't.
She must have known
it would have told her
how little she knew
about the whole thing,
about everything,
miles and miles of everything.
Who wants such a revelation.
She was handling life just fine

back in West Virginia.
There was not a day
she had more questions than answers.
The ocean went on too far
for Ludie,
who preferred seeing only the next ridge
out her kitchen window,
where trees grew whose names she knew
and a creek flowed,
small enough.

Everybody in Ludie's house smoked.
When the family gathered around the kitchen table
(which Rupe had pulled from the Halsteads' barn
and shellacked
and now was pretty enough for rich people)
and poured their coffee
and got a piece of whatever sweet was in the house,
there was afterward
some serious puffing going on.
Matches and lighters going back and forth,
then all those good, deep drags
moving around the table.
Nothing better.
Though she did not smoke,
Ludie never minded.
She just lived and let live.
And besides,
what else would have kept everybody at the table
talking so long,
the coffee mugs refilling
and the conversation getting better and better?

The grandchildren would pull in
whatever bench or stool they could
find to sit on,
and in that fog of secondhand smoke
learn about Rupe walking halfway
from Alabama to West Virginia
with a great big hole in his shoe,
or Uncle Varn
starting up the Missionary Baptist Church out the road,
or just how far the women had to go for water
in that one coal camp.
If Marlboro had been smart,
it would have shown this—
Ludie's family—
instead of that lonely old cowboy
with no one to talk to
and not even a piece of cake.
Cigarettes had kept Ludie's family talking for years.
Without them, it might have been just
the evening news and *Wheel of Fortune* after supper.
No children ever knowing
about Uncle Varn.

In her last months of high school,

Ludie's granddaughter

started dating the only rich boy in her senior class.

Ludie had never met the boy.

But she knew who he was.

Everybody did.

His father was a mine owner

and had made a lot of money from it.

Now they lived

in a big, fancy house

in the first gated community

that part of the country had ever seen.

To drive in,

people had to be cleared

by a man in uniform

sitting in a small brick building

with classic white trim around its windows.

Who knew what was beyond.

Country people

making ends meet

never did or would.
But Ludie's granddaughter,
shy and pretty,
started dating that boy
and in the front bucket seat
of a new metallic Camaro
would glide by that small brick building,
past that uniform,
as if her grandfather Rupe had never once
picked at a seam of coal,
desperate to earn a living
in someone else's mine.
Ludie's granddaughter
never spoke much about the boy to Ludie,
maybe knowing full well the dangers
of discussing the rich in Ludie's house.
But she seemed happy enough
and said only
that the family was nice.
Then when graduation day came
and Ludie and all the

aunts and uncles and cousins

went to see this granddaughter

walk that stage,

tears in their eyes,

and the rich boy's parents did not show,

did not show,

even Ludie's low estimation of the wealthy

was outdone.

It troubled her for days.

Evidently they had gone out to dinner instead.

And when that boy's uncle

became governor of West Virginia,

years after Ludie's granddaughter

and the boy had parted ways,

Ludie never once cared

that her own clan

might have been a part of that,

if things had worked out differently.

She saw the name in the paper every day now

and did not once care

that she had no direct line

to the governor's mansion.

Though Ludie did wonder now and then
whether anyone in the governor's family
had found the time to attend
his commencement.

$\mathcal{A}$ cherry tree spread its boughs
beside Ludie and Rupe's house in the country.
It was big
and the children stayed in its branches
all summer.
Then Rupe got a notion that lightning
might strike that tree,
that one tree,
setting the house afire
and who knows where they'd be then.
So he cut it down.
A beautiful, healthy, fruit-giving tree.
And some years later,
intuiting his own death,
he told his sons
to cut down all the apple trees
in the yard behind the house.
How would Ludie
deal with all those apples
fallen and rotting on the ground
after he'd gone?

So they cut them down.
And it seemed to Ludie
that little by little
life was packing her up for that long journey home.
The chickens and chicken pens gone.
The hogs gone from the hog lot.
No beagle tied to a doghouse.
No doghouse.
Rupe left her
one small apple tree
outside the kitchen window
where she liked to feed the birds.
After she was too old to get the seed out,
her sons did it for her.
But she knew
this would not always be so.
Good-bye had started
with one tree,
and good-bye would end
with another,
its apples fallen,
and the birds all flown.

Ardis and Ozella Boggs
had been friends of Ludie's family for years.
They lived up White Oak Road
in a small gray house with black shutters,
carefully maintained,
a glider on the front porch,
enormous sunflowers and roses in the yard,
and cabbages in the large, lush garden.
They raised three girls,
one went up to the university
and earned a doctorate
then died in a plane crash.
Ozella went blind.
And Ardis...
Ardis was accused
by a little girl at the Missionary Baptist Church
of touching her inappropriately.
Ardis had been a fixture of that church
for thirty years.
Summers, the congregation
had climbed the hill on his land

up into the cherry groves,

and with tin pails in their hands,

had picked cherries all day long

to take home and bake pies

and can jellies

and just eat them plain in the hand,

fingers dark red

with the sweetness.

Ardis had been a fixture.

And when this happened,

this story with the little girl,

he was asked not to come back.

Sin was one thing.

But this was something else.

Ludie and Rupe and all the rest

continued driving on past Ardis and Ozella's house

on their way somewhere every week.

But no one was ever seen sitting out on that glider,

the sunflowers growing,

the roses

heavy with neglect.

Every one of Ludie's children and grandchildren
who went to college came back different.
Every one.
Ludie still loved them, but they irritated her.
They'd always come back
against things she'd done all her life.
They stopped eating meat,
they stopped going to church,
they lost that hillbilly accent
they'd left with.
The girls always liked those New York boys
they met at college,
and they'd bring them out to the house.
A never-ending flow of New York boys.
What were these boys doing going to
West Virginia colleges in the first place?
Weren't they smart enough
for their own colleges?
Rupe would fix up the sleep sofa
for whichever boy it was,
and they'd endure the visit as best they could,

but it was a challenge;

the boy was probably on drugs anyway

and why was it country boys just didn't appeal

to the women in this family?

Ludie cooked proudly for the New Yorkers,

she could see that her starry-eyed girls

wanted to give these boys a real country experience.

So she served up the cornbread and

pinto beans and fried chicken

and reminded herself

that each boy was,

after all,

some mother's son,

and here he was waiting to be fed,

and even if he was on drugs

he'd still need supper.

A couple of those New York boys

actually turned into in-laws,

and Ludie and Rupe actually liked them,

especially the one who

called Rupe "Pop"

and teased him about his shiny head.

That New Yorker was all right.
And when he fathered
two baby girls,
beautiful grandbabies for Ludie to once again
rock to sleep,
she forgot all about where he was from
and what he might have smoked.
She loved him.
He called her "Mom,"
and she was.

Yvonne from up the road
did Ludie's hair for her
when it was time for a cut and a perm.
Yvonne did hair in people's houses,
so she'd come into Ludie's kitchen
while Rupe got busy with something in the garage,
and she'd spread out her little tissue papers
and plastic snap-rollers,
her white squeeze bottles
and cotton balls,
her combs and scissors
and the mirror so Ludie could see the back,
and she'd get started.
Yvonne was a talker,
she had to be,
getting this intimate with people in their kitchens,
and she gave Ludie a lot of information
most of which was useless to Ludie
but which she was happy to gather,
for she didn't get up the road
as often as she used to

and who knew so much was going on up there.
By the time she'd dunked her head
for the last time in the kitchen sink,
Ludie had enough gossip to gnaw on for several weeks,
and as Yvonne combed her out
she wanted to somehow tell Yvonne
what a time this had been,
what a morning
for Ludie,
all this excitement in her kitchen,
and that sharp tang of curl neutralizer in the air
making her feel younger and prettier
and not so thick as one gets to feel,
living in the country
with beans for supper
and the soaps
starting every day at one.

When Ludie was twenty-two,

she walked on water.

That's what they all said.

What happened was she was on a picnic

with her father and Rupe

and her small son.

Her father had brought along a rifle.

This was rural Alabama.

And somehow

while the old man was feeding his line

into the water,

the small son knocked the gun over,

shot the old man in the back.

And it was Ludie

who had to get back to town

for help,

while Rupe tried to keep the man alive

and the small son screamed.

Why Ludie wore heels that day

who can say.

Vanity.

She was twenty-two
and beautiful.
In heels she was to run
through the woods
and across the train trestle above the river
into town for help.
If only someone had been there with a camera.
If only someone
had documented it.
For Ludie made it through the woods fast enough
in those heels.
But the train trestle
would be impossible to run in those shoes.
Ludie knew it.
So instead she crossed the river below.
Ludie crossed that wide river somehow,
though she could not,
had never been able to,
swim.
She crossed that wide river
and, soaked through, made it to town,
where, hysterical, she told someone

the old man had shot the small son,
she got it backward,
and then she fainted.
The old man lived,
for it was buckshot in that gun, not a bullet,
and though it made a mess of his back,
the gun did not take out anything vital.
Ludie never told her
grandchildren this story.
Ludie never told them
much of anything about the days when
she was young and beautiful and
could walk on water.
They could not imagine her so.
So why bother?
What happens when someone who is old
still sees
out of the same eyes?
The world is the same world,
and you are still you,
and if not for the eyes of others
looking back at you,

you'd never know you'd stopped being
twenty-two and beautiful,
you'd never know there are things
you don't deserve now,
now that you are old.
Take away the breathless young men,
take away the solicitous shoe salesman,
the envious women,
the adoring children,
and replace these with people who
do not really believe or care
that you had
beautiful, clear skin and shiny blond curls,
lovely legs,
and that in the night
you made your man happy.
Ludie walked on water when she was young,
but she never told her grandchildren.

One of Ludie's daughters

was born again in her thirties.

No one could have guessed

this would be the one to go off the deep end.

She'd lived in New York City out of college,

marched in antiwar rallies,

wore those long granny coats

when they were all the rage.

She even married an ex-junkie.

Then the two of them

moved back to West Virginia,

set up a modular home beside Ludie,

and started having kids.

When the oldest boy was four,

and the youngest was two,

that's when Ludie's daughter repented of her sins

out at the Missionary Baptist Church

Uncle Varn had started up decades ago.

There was a young preacher

preaching there,

and he had a power.

And before long
Ludie's daughter had stopped wearing long pants
and had started telling everybody
they were going to Hell.
Imagine the strain on that marriage.
An ex-junkie from the Bronx
and a born-again Christian hillbilly.
It didn't last.
He moved out, found a reasonable woman
and remarried.
Ludie's daughter's rapture ran its course,
she went to theology school,
and then, for whatever reason,
stopped going to church altogether.
Ludie, all this time, watched and waited,
believing in the Lord
but not about to get mixed up with
crazy evangelicals or theologians.
When another of her children was saved in his fifties,
Ludie held her breath
and kept on wearing long pants.
But his conversion was a quiet one.

He didn't mention Hell

unless some politician pissed him off.

Now here was a Christian

Ludie could live with.

In Alabama there had been tornadoes
and even after she moved to West Virginia
and was assured again and again
that there were no tornadoes there,
don't worry,
they can't jump the mountains,
Ludie never trusted the weather.
And when the storm clouds brewed,
she'd start unplugging everything
and bringing the children in,
an eye on the basement, just in case.
She'd lived through one tornado in Alabama.
The woman next door had run for the cellar,
didn't make it,
so she grabbed on to a tree,
and when it was all over,
the tree was there
and the woman was there, too,
stark naked,
clothes blown right off.
Ludie never trusted the weather.

Her children picked up on this,
and when they were grown,
they were the same way.
Unplugged everything.
Wouldn't touch the phone.
Preferred homes with basements.
Well, survivalism
is not such a bad thing.
Golfers are struck
by lightning every day
and Ludie might say they had it coming,
being out there in the first place.
Though Ludie believed in God and no accidents.
It was a paradox to her.
How much to trust God
and how much to trust Ludie.
She kept a cellar full of canned corn
and beets
and tomatoes,
two big bins of potatoes,
some pickled eggs,
and there was always enough flour in the kitchen,

enough lard for biscuits.

Ludie would take care of Ludie

and let God

worry about the golfers.

Only one time did she think there might not be enough,

only once did she have doubts about surviving.

Rupe got hurt in the mine when some slate fell on him,

and a couple inches more to the right

might have paralyzed him.

He couldn't work,

and there they were,

by that time living in a little house

way out in the country—

the coal camp shut down

years earlier—

living out in the country

and Rupe,

the breadwinner,

the driver,

the woodchopper,

the man,

flat on his back.

And this is when Ludie
learned to love America.
Because the government stepped in.
And while it would be years before the
government took a good hard look at what
coal was doing to men's lungs
while the wealthy fed their furnaces with it,
the government did accept some responsibility
for not letting people starve.
So Ludie and Rupe got Commodities:
bulk packages of flour,
sugar,
cheese,
powdered milk,
peanut butter,
courtesy America.
And this kept them and their family fed
that winter
until Rupe could roll out of bed
and hunt rabbits again,
plant a garden,
drive out for a couple pounds of flour.

There was still some shame clinging to him,
shame he'd not gotten out of the way
of that slate quick enough,
shame that he'd had to take Commodities.
But he'd been working in the mines since he was nine,
he and Ludie had kept six babies
fat and healthy,
and if ever anybody was owed
a free block of American cheese,
it was these two.
Still, it shook them to need it
and from then on they kept a tighter hold
to the little money they had
and extra potatoes in the cellar
and didn't buy
much of anything new
until 1969 when the government finally
squared up and paid all the dying coal miners
what it thought they were owed
for their lungs.
Rupe got some money,
enough to buy a nice china cabinet for Ludie,

a couple recliner chairs,

and a better car.

But by then he was on his way down from emphysema

and would be laid out for a year in pain,

struggling for air,

Ludie up all night with hot towels for his back

and prayers to God.

And all the

unplugged appliances

and bins of potatoes

in the world

would not save them this time.

In her young days of homemaking,
Ludie's breakfasts were an event.
Fried eggs,
fried bacon,
pancakes,
biscuits.
She was famous for her biscuits.
She kept a tin pan of self-rising flour
in the kitchen cabinet,
and when it came time to make biscuits,
she brought it out
with the can of Crisco.
She eyeballed a gob of Crisco,
and with her right hand
mashed it into the center of that pan of flour.
She added a little buttermilk and kept mashing
until she had a nice bit of soft dough
coming together.
Then with both hands floured,
she rolled pieces of that dough into small balls,
squashed them flat,

and placed these into an old black biscuit pan.

She brushed the tops of all the biscuits with bacon grease

left over from breakfast

and popped that pan into the oven for ten minutes,

450 degrees.

Everybody who spent any time at Ludie's house

asked her to make them some biscuits.

When one grandchild

got strange about food,

there were only three things

people could get her to eat:

Cookie Crisp cereal,

McDonald's french fries,

and Ludie's biscuits.

In her old age

Ludie got tired of making biscuits.

For breakfast

she had half of a grapefruit

and a boiled egg

and was done with it.

Those who missed the biscuits

tried to make a batch themselves,

hauling that pan of self-rising flour out of Ludie's cabinet
when they stopped by.
But their biscuits never measured up,
and next time Ludie just did it for them.
Eventually the pan stayed in the cabinet.
And if anybody craved biscuits,
they had to go to the Big Oak Restaurant out at the mall,
where some young girl in a checkered apron
would bring forth a plate of eggs and bacon
and the biggest biscuits anybody had ever seen.
One bite, though,
and nothing but a sigh of disappointment,
coupled with a keen understanding
that when Ludie died,
genius
was going with her.

The worst thing that ever happened to Ludie

was loneliness,

and this occurred only in her final years,

so one may say

she had a lucky life.

She did not outlive her children,

was never in a hospital,

and did not fear death.

But loneliness,

had she known it was coming,

might have destroyed her.

Ludie had been deprived, yes.

Of a mother.

Of enough money.

Of certain opportunities.

But Ludie had never been lonely.

And how rich such a life must seem

to the wandering lost of this generation,

this modern one.

Automatic garage doors swallowing people up,

the desolation of divorce,

and eating alone at the coffee table.
Ludie had someone to sleep with
for the first seventy years.
First her sister.
Then her husband.
Never a night alone
until Rupe started dying
and was taken to the hospital to finish it.
And his passing
opened that door just a crack,
the door toward loneliness,
but there were more grandchildren,
the neighbors dropping in,
and church—
as long as the preacher
wasn't too bent on Hell—
so Ludie learned to sleep alone in a bed at night,
the only person in the house,
the quiet hum of the furnace
for company.
She was never afraid
alone in that house.

The only thing she
should have feared—
loneliness—
was such an impossibility in her mind
that it couldn't keep her up nights.
But when she was ninety,
yes, ninety,
sitting alone in the living room,
eyes too bad to read,
ears too bad for television,
Rupe dead,
old neighbors dead,
grandchildren gone,
children in their retirement years with
problems of their own,
at ninety, Ludie was finally alone,
and in the living room she sat for hours
in silence
remembering
the car trips to Virginia,
the sewing circle,
the Sunday dinners,

the dominoes,
the prayer meetings,
the canning,
the babies asleep on the floor,
Rupe, whispering in the dark,
and, at ninety,
she knew loneliness
for the first time
as the clock ticked
and she lived on
while everything around her
passed away.

Rupe had been dead awhile
and Ludie had gotten used to living alone
when the man-woman
built a house next door.
That's what Ludie called her:
the man-woman.
Ludie had never seen the likes of her,
and Ludie was impressed.
For this woman could do anything.
She built her own house.
Built it from scratch,
put in the windows,
roofed it,
and added a deck with some curlicues.
For starters.
She fixed her own truck when it broke down.
She planted a garden just thick with
beans and tomatoes.
She put a pretty little picket fence around that.
She did all this *and* she also worked
as a dental assistant *and* she also raised a

boy by herself *and* she also made time

to come over and see what needed doing

at Ludie's house.

Ludie had never seen such a woman.

Then one day some money went missing

from Ludie's pocketbook.

It was enough money to be noticed.

Ludie always left her door unlocked.

Anyone could have come in and helped themselves

while she was walking out for the mail.

Some money went missing,

and after a few inquiries it turned out

the money had been taken by the

man-woman's boy.

His name was Leon.

He rode ATVs.

Leon was a husky boy,

about fourteen,

and pure country.

Ludie was so sad about it.

A child headed in the wrong direction.

Leon came over and apologized to her,

the man-woman standing on the deck

to make sure he did it.

Ludie hated this.

Not the apology, but the tragedy,

the blamed tragedy of it all,

for the boy's father was nowhere to be seen

and even though the man-woman

the boy had for a mother

worked hard to make a home,

a boy needed a whole man,

not a half of one.

Rupe had kept his boys in line

and not one of them ever stole a dime.

And Ludie knew if it had been her by herself

raising their boys,

she'd never have known how to make them

do a thing

if they didn't want to do it;

you could take a switch to a child's legs only so long.

Sooner or later

he'd be too big,

and then he'd need a man to measure up to,

a man who'd put up
with none of that foolishness.
Leon was a heartbreak to Ludie,
for she knew that he was deep down a good boy,
he just didn't believe it.
Leon didn't believe it.
And that man-woman could fix a lot,
but she'd likely never make that
one sorrowful repair.

Rupe was placed in
one of those mausoleum drawers
out at the Green Ridge Cemetery
after he died.
This man who spent his life underground
now was destined
to spend eternity above it.
Ludie would never have chosen a drawer—
nor Rupe—
but when he got sick
and things looked bad,
one of the daughters begged them to buy one.
She worried that her father would die in
the middle of winter
with six inches of ice plus two feet of snow
over those rolling hills of the Green Ridge
and no way to break through
and bury a man.
She could not bear the thought of him
in a freezer at the funeral parlor,
waiting on a thaw.

Why she was at peace about

a drawer at the mausoleum is a puzzle.

But people are funny about death.

Ludie and Rupe contacted the cemetery office

and bought their drawers—

their "crypts" as the industry

liked to call them—

and the daughter slept better.

Then Rupe died, as expected,

and Ludie paid her visits to him out at

Building 2.

It was always chilly inside,

cold marble walls and floors,

cheap blue carpet in a patch near the middle,

and never anyone there,

in spite of the long hallway of the departed.

The mausoleum remained cold and silent every season.

In spring,

when all the other dead were out enjoying

the sound of birds

and the smell of soft new grass above their heads.

In fall,

when the trees blessed them with color.
And, of course,
in winter,
when Building 2 sat in its dim loneliness
as outside, the mountains filled with snow
and the sky opened blue.
Ludie visited Rupe regularly,
exchanging the artificial silk flowers in his assigned urn
according to the season,
but she never stayed long,
never was inspired to linger or say much,
if anything,
and when she finally stepped back out to the car,
was ready to go,
to go anywhere
where there might be a bit of air,
a ray of light,
some promise of a world
continuing.

Ludie and her sister, Trula,
had been through a lot
and they were close.
They weren't much alike, though.
Ludie was strong and good-looking,
Trula was too thin
and she smoked constantly,
giving her that throaty deep voice
moviegoers love to hear.
Trula was dependent.
When her husband, Cleo, was alive,
he took care of her,
and after he died,
her children took care of her,
dropping off her meals
even when she was perfectly capable
of cooking for herself.
But Trula had gotten hooked
on the CB radio her policeman son had given her,
and she didn't have much time for cooking.
Day after day she sat by that thing,

couldn't miss a word,
what if something happened
without her?
That CB radio ate her up,
and it just drove Ludie crazy when she visited
and Trula did nothing but sit there all day with it on.
Ludie missed the times they'd
canned tomatoes together
and sewed
and worked in the yard a little.
She read her romance book
while Trula listened for
who was doing what where.
But she loved Trula.
Loved her sister.
They were close.
When Rupe died
Trula carried on worse than Ludie,
like it was her own husband,
Trula loved so deeply.
Then when Cleo died,
it was all anyone could do

to get Trula to let them bury him.

Trula kept him home, dead in a casket,

for more days than she probably should have.

Trula was something.

She loved to sit in Ludie's kitchen

and smoke

and laugh about outrageous things,

like just what did those gay men do

when they were together,

she couldn't figure it out.

Trula was bawdy.

Eighty pounds,

wrinkled,

funny as hell.

When she died,

Ludie made it to the funeral,

but after that she never went to Virginia again,

never went back to see Trula's family,

which was also her own.

She couldn't take it.

Ludie was strong,

she could take a lot.

But her sister not being there in that house,
the full hard truth of that
would be too much.
So she stayed home in West Virginia
and it was like any other time between visits.
She'd see Trula soon enough.
Just had to wait a bit on the weather.
And get a few things done
around the house.

When Ludie was eighty-four,

one of her granddaughters died.

No child had yet been lost in Ludie's family.

At eighty-four,

she thought she'd skirted

the worst of things.

But this granddaughter,

in her first apartment,

asleep with her boyfriend and her cat,

died.

Not alone.

All three were lost.

This was some comfort to Ludie.

That the lovely girl had not been alone.

The child's mother and brother found her.

The carbon monoxide still in every corner.

The horror of this cannot be spoken.

Ludie did the best she could

for her agonized daughter.

But at eighty-four,

she could do little but sit softly

in her daughter's house
those first few weeks,
absorbing the pain,
helping with the laundry.
Mornings were hardest.
Maybe Ludie wished she hadn't lived so long.
That she hadn't made it to eighty-four and this.
And wouldn't she have loved
to trade places with her granddaughter.
An old woman burying this girl was not right.
People say the Bible helps,
times like these,
but Ludie did not reach for it.
She knew her Bible
and there was nothing in it for now.
Maybe later,
when words meant something.
Her granddaughter died
and her daughter would never be the same.
That gray grief would always be there
inside her eyes.
Ludie went on back home to her own bed,

where she lay in the night
missing Rupe like she never had.
She was so alone,
trying to hold people together in one piece,
trying to do it by herself,
and she could not falter,
it was not her turn.
The family wasn't ready for it.
But she was so worn out
being the steady center
people clung to
when the walls fell away.
And she was glad
folks didn't live past one hundred.
Life would just make more death.
And Ludie
had had
enough.

Back when Ludie was young
and expecting her sixth child,
the novelty of choosing names
had worn off,
so she struck a deal with a neighbor woman that,
in exchange for the neighbor's Christmas cactus,
Ludie would name the sixth baby
after her.
And, sure enough,
the baby was a girl
and promptly named Shelma.
Ludie's other two daughters had been named
Fleda and Bernice.
Somehow an ear for beautiful names
had escaped Ludie.
All of Ludie's children were crazy about Rupe,
but their feelings toward Ludie
were more complicated.
They called her "Mother,"
instead of "Mama," for example,
which sends a certain message.

Maybe this was because
Ludie was the one with the switch.
Ludie was never shy with a switch
and no child escaped the sting of it.
But it was only a twig from a tree,
after all.
It wasn't personal,
it wasn't vicious,
the way words can be.
Ludie never did that.
She never tore her children down that way,
and maybe that's why,
when they all grew up and left,
they all, except one,
came back.
The one exception was the eldest son
who married a woman so exquisitely bitter
that no one was much disappointed
when they settled in Cleveland.
The other children, though,
they circled back.

The boys had been in the service;
two girls became teachers;
the other, a nurse.
These coal miner's children
had pulled up their proverbial bootstraps
and now took to living quite nicely
with indoor plumbing
and satellite.
Ludie had made soldiers and
teachers and nurses
for the world.
So what did she finally believe in,
as the years rolled by?
What did she finally believe?
When Ludie was young
she thought she knew
what was right.
She had been bigoted.
A white coal-camp girl from Alabama,
one would expect it.
She had no love of Jews or Italians.

Then one of her children married a Jew,
another married an Italian.
What did Ludie believe in, finally,
as the years rolled away
and scripture revealed itself to her
in a new world?
She might have said she believed less in the Bible
and more in a cup of coffee
and an open front door.
For this is what mattered most to her.
This is what everyone found—
the children and the grandchildren
who would eventually come to her
pulling behind them some person
they weren't supposed to love.
They found a cup of coffee
and a smile
and an open front door.
Ludie had seen too much of life
to waste any time
telling others how to live.

One young granddaughter
had already died and who knew
how many more
would pass on unexpected.
She would not waste any time
telling others how to live.
So everyone circled back.
The two little neighbor girls
from the house over the hill came by often,
choosing a peppermint candy from the bowl
and sitting in Ludie's kitchen,
telling her about school.
When their dog died,
the oldest girl came to Ludie and
cried an hour at that table.
Ludie's granddaughter's old boyfriend
brought some frozen squirrel he'd hunted
and spent the afternoon
telling her all the mistakes he'd made.
This is how it went in Ludie's house.
And until she went into the nursing home, at ninety-three,

the morning after she
tried to go out in the snow
looking for...who was it?...
this is how it went.
She still loved the Bible,
but she thought less about God
and more about the front door.

What would Ludie have thought,
at age twenty-two,
running through the woods in heels,
if she had known
she'd die one day in a small narrow bed
in a nursing home,
stricken children by her side,
her house already stripped and empty and
Medicaid's padlock on the front door.
Would she have said then, at twenty-two,
"I want to live to a ripe old age."
Or would she have chosen, then and there,
when she would end it.
Maybe she'd go when Rupe died.
She'd be seventy—what could
be worth staying for?
Or maybe she'd go when she was eighty.
Just head off into the woods to get a Christmas
tree and never turn back.
Eighty was a nice round age.
But Ludie didn't choose.

She let time do it for her.
So she went into the nursing home,
and for two years,
she knew she was missing something
but didn't know what it was,
knew she wanted to go home,
but didn't really,
she'd forgotten why.
The children came by
and helped her into the bathroom
and changed her clothes
and showed her
where the potatoes were on the tray.
Sometimes a grandchild
came by and held her hand.
And Mrs. Cook, in the next bed over,
breathing on that big machine.
Ludie was seven miles from home.
Seven miles.
The birds were gathering in her apple tree,
fog drifting in,
the sky filling with stars.

Seven miles.

She wasn't lonely anymore.

People in and out all day,

Rupe would be glad of that.

When they were young they had

played Setback

with Trula and Cleo,

Elva and Harleigh,

Maudie and Bill.

Cards all night in Ludie's kitchen

and the laughing

and good hot coffee.

Then everyone to bed,

Ludie and Rupe in that solid brown bed

they'd had since the coal camp.

Rupe had lost most of his hearing young,

and he'd leave his hearing aid in the

dish by the bed.

But they talked quietly, late,

the two of them,

and he could always hear her.

He could hear Ludie,

his wife,

and she was still beautiful

and he was tall and kind.

In the nursing home, when she was ninety-five,

Ludie would look for him to stop by,

she'd ask her children

have you seen your father,

she knew he was stopping by.

They'd have coffee and pound cake,

then he'd read the paper and

she'd read her romance book.

They'd lock up.

Turn down the heat.

Climb into bed and talk.

Ludie waited

while everyone came and went,

came and went,

came and went,

then finally,

one morning

just before dawn,

Rupe stopped by.

It was a beautiful morning when Ludie died,
just the kind of April morning she loved.
She'd get up early and go out to the kitchen
to make a pot of coffee,
the sun rising just over the mountains,
and dew on the grass.
It was so quiet these mornings.
Ludie would sit at the round kitchen table
Rupe had pulled from a barn years ago
and watch the birds at the feeder.
The trees all glistened silver in the light
and the world was
calm as heaven.
Was it any wonder, then, that Ludie
chose to die just before dawn?
How else would she have
caught the morning in this,
her final moment on the earth?
She would have wanted to take one last look
at the small white house in the mountains,
at the dirt road which had always led her home.

She would have wanted to say good-bye.
Somewhere Ludie was going to find
everything she had ever lost.
And she would go looking...
just as soon as Rupe finished his coffee,
and all the birds had flown.